Buzz and Jump! Jump!

'Buzz' and 'Jump! Jump!'
An original concept by Alice Hemming

Illustrated by Louise Forshaw

Published by MAVERICK ARTS PUBLISHING LTD

Studio 3A, City Business Centre, 6 Brighton Road,

Horsham, West Sussex, RH13 5BB

+44 (0)1403 256941

A CIP catalogue record for this book is available at the British Library.

ISBN 978-1-84886-250-0

Maverick
arts publishing
www.maverickbooks.co.uk

This book is rated as: Red Band (Guided Reading)
This story is decodable at Letters and Sounds Phase 2.

Buzz and Jump! Jump!

By
Alice Hemming

Illustrated by
Louise Forshaw

The Letter B

Trace the lower and upper case letter with a finger. Sound out the letter.

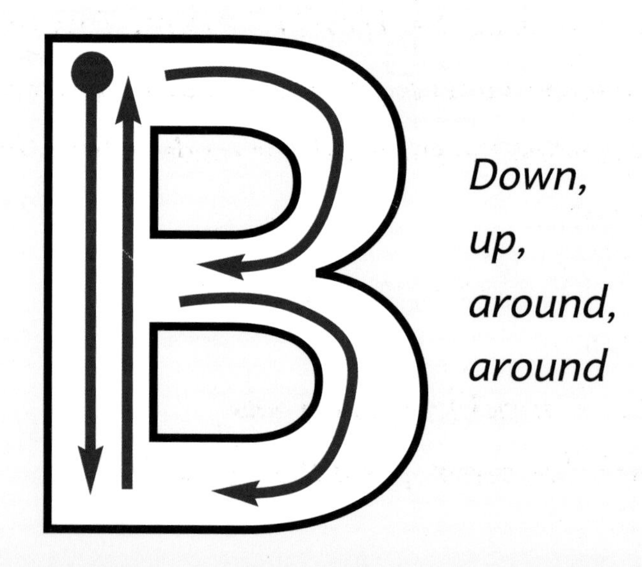

Some words to familiarise:

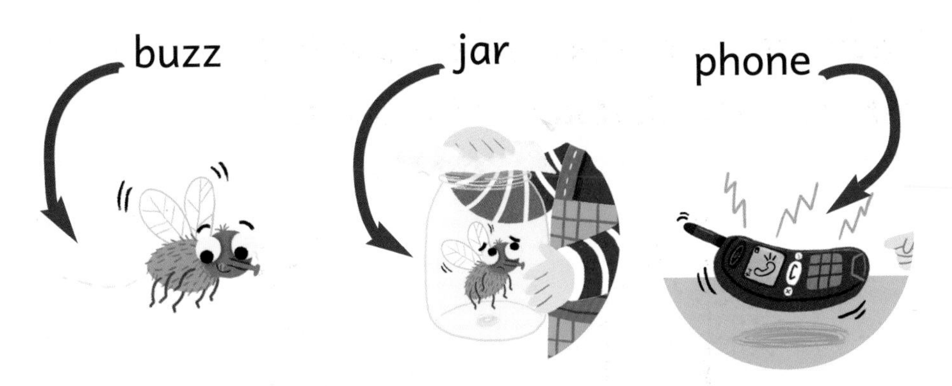

High-frequency words:

it is in the

Tips for Reading 'Buzz'

- Practise the tricky words listed above before reading the story.

- If the reader struggles with any of the other words, ask them to look for sounds they know in the word. Encourage them to sound out the words and help them read the words if necessary.

- After reading the story, ask the reader what other things there are that buzz.

Fun Activity

Take turns to make an animal noise.

Can the other person guess the animal?'

Buzz

Buzz, buzz.

It is a bug.
Get it!

Buzz, buzz.

Got it!

It is in the jar.

Let it out!

Buzz, buzz.

Buzz, buzz.

Buzz, buzz.

Buzz, buzz.

Mum! It is your phone.

The Letter J

Trace the lower and upper case letter with a finger. Sound out the letter.

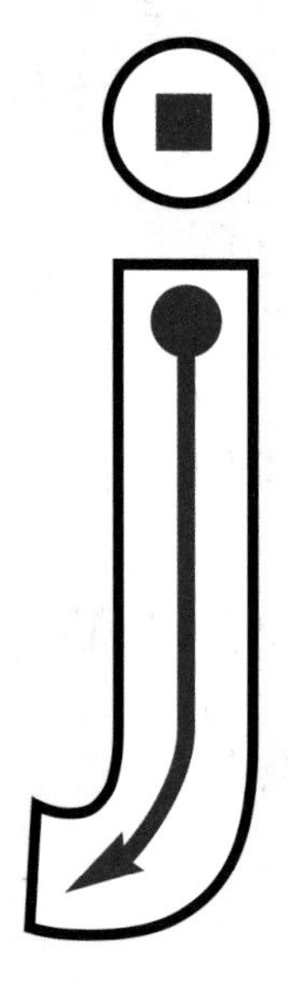

Down,
around,
lift,
dot

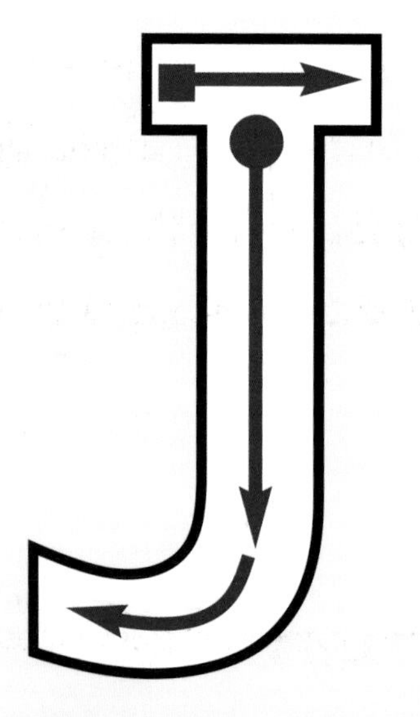

Down,
around,
lift,
across

Practise the tricky words before reading the story:

High-frequency words:

in a I am the at up
no to off you

Tips for Reading 'Jump! Jump!'

- Practise the tricky words listed above before reading the story.

- If the reader struggles with any of the other words, ask them to look for sounds they know in the word. Encourage them to sound out the words and help them read the words if necessary.

- After reading the story, ask the reader why Ken doesn't go to the party.

Fun Activity

Play a jumping game. Who can jump for the longest?

Jump! Jump!

Ken is a kangaroo.

He jumps a lot.

I am the best at jumping!

Ken jumps up the hill.

Hop on the bus, Ken!

No, I want
to jump!

Ken jumps in the library.

Ken jumps in the shops.

Ken huffs and puffs.
Ken is hot and red.

We are off to
a party, Ken.
Will you come?

No, I want to jump...

...into bed.

- Pink
- Red (End of Yr R)
- Yellow
- Blue
- Green
- Orange
- Turquoise (End of Yr 1)
- Purple
- Gold
- White (End of Yr 2)
- Lime

Book Bands for Guided Reading

The Institute of Education book banding system is made up of twelve colours, which reflect the level of reading difficulty. The bands are assigned by taking into account the content, the language style, the layout and phonics.

Children learn at different speeds but the colour chart shows the levels of progression with the national expectation shown in brackets. To learn more visit the IoE website: www.ioe.ac.uk.

All of these books have been book banded for guided reading to the industry standard and edited by a leading educational consultant.

For more titles visit: www.maverickbooks.co.uk/early-readers